THREE LITTLE KITTENS

(and one little mouse!)

BARBARA McCLINTOCK

SCHOLASTIC PRESS / NEW YORK

"Three Little Kittens" is an English-language nursery rhyme that possibly has roots in British folk tradition. A version of the poem appeared in print in 1827 in the *Eton Miscellany*. Eliza Lee Follen later enhanced and popularized this poem as part of *Little Songs, for Little Boys and Girls* (1833), and it's often attributed to her. But in fact, it was later recorded by her as "traditional." It has a Roud Folk Song Index number of 16150.

LIBRARY OF CONGRESS CATALOGING-IN-PUBLICATION DATA

Names: McClintock, Barbara, author, illustrator. Title: Three little kittens / by Barbara McClintock, Other titles: Mother Goose. Description: First edition. | New York : Scholastic Press, 2020. | Summary: A humorous reimagining of the classic nursery rhyme about three kittens, who lose, find, and ultimately mess up their mittens—and share their pie with one hungry mouse. Identifiers: LCCN 2018060395 | ISBN 9781338125870 (alk. paper) Subjects: LCSH: Three little kittens—Adaptations—Juvenile fiction. | Kittens—Juvenile fiction. | Mice—Juvenile fiction. | Nursery rhymes. | Humorous stories. | CYAC: Cats—Fiction. | Animals—Infancy—Fiction. | Characters in literature—Fiction. | Humorous stories. | LCGFT: Nursery rhymes. | Humorous fiction.Classification: LCC PZ7.M47841418 Th 2020 | DDC [E]--dc23

10 9 8 7 6 5 4 3 2 1   20 21 22 23 24

Printed in Malaysia 108

First edition, April 2020

Barbara McClintock's drawings were created with pencil, watercolor, and gouache on Arches hot press watercolor paper. The hand lettering and voice balloons were done by Barbara McClintock. The display type and text type was set in Rand Shag Expert Lounge. The book was printed on 130 gsm Lumisilk matt art paper and bound at Tien Wah Press. Production was overseen by Catherine Weening. Manufacturing was supervised by Shannon Rice. The book was art directed by David Saylor, designed by Barbara McClintock and Charles Kreloff, and edited by Dianne Hess. With special thanks to Karen Van Rossem, Suzanne Alteri, Barbara Beth Schulman, and Anne Pellowski for finding and verifying sources that led us to early versions of this poem.

To Walter Chandoha

One morning, three little kittens were playing outside.

But they *had* lost their mittens.

And they began to cry.

The three little kittens

they found their mittens

and they began to smile.

The three little kittens

put on their mittens.

And soon ate up the pie.

Then they began to sigh.

The three little kittens

they washed their mittens.

Then they hung them out to dry.

Oh, Mother dear.
Look here! Look here!
Our mittens we have washed.

What? Washed your mittens? You good little Kittens.
You are the best kittens any mother ever had!

And they all had some pie.